LEGENDS OF
LEEPER HOLLER

NORMAN MCFADDEN

1

LEGENDS OF LEEPER HOLLER

LEGENDS OF
LEEPER HOLLER

NORMAN MCFADDEN

POLSTON HOUSE
PUBLISHING

LEGENDS OF LEEPER HOLLER

Published by Polston House Publishing LLC
www.PolstonHouse.com

Artwork used from public domain.
Book design copyright © 2018 by Polston House Publishing, LLC. All rights reserved.

Published in the United States of America

In loving memory of my Mom and Dad.

Otis Mcfadden

October 30th 1921- October 9th 1988

Alice Mcfadden

April 28th 1928- December 14th 1984

CONTENTS

1 Grandpa the Moonshiner……...............11

2 Elbow Room……...……….................19

3 Doc Hurley and the James Gang.......23

4 The Joke that Killed……...……........35

5 The Nipper Woods Bigfoot…...…......41

6 The First Day of School……............51

7 The Boy on all Fours……...............59

8 Burnt Ends……………………........65

9 The Boy With a Girl's Name….…......77

10 Bum's Cave……………………......83

About the Author…………...…….........95

LEGENDS OF LEEPER HOLLER

NOTE FROM THE AUTHOR

I would like to give special thanks to Polston House publishing. Having had the confidence in my ability, to help me make this dream come true. I like giving credit where the credit is due. The true credit is in God giving me The chance to have such an amazing childhood with a loving family. Giving me the ability to write about them. Finally, I'd like to thank you for going out and buying my book. I know you're going to enjoy the Legends of Leeper Holler!

LEGENDS OF LEEPER HOLLER

NOTE FROM THE EDITOR

At the request of the Author, this book has been published in the original written form. Which includes country grammar, Hillbilly slang and backwoods euphemisms. While there remains a national standard for written English in the publishing industry, and against the initial judgment of the staff, "*we dinnit figger it would hurt nuttin dis one time.*"

LEGENDS OF LEEPER HOLLER

The Adventures of Little Mac

1

GRANDPA THE MOONSHINER

It is 1964, and I'm a ten year old boy. My name is Little Mac and I live in the backwoods of Southeast Missouri. In a sleepy little town that lay along the mighty Black River, called Leeper. I actually live in Leeper Holler. I have adventures every day, since my mom always said, "Life is an adventure, so get out there and find it". I took her words to heart, and I get out there and live my life to its fullest every day.

Tomorrow is Saturday and my cousin Junior is spending the night with me. It's always a lot of fun running around with him. Because he is more than a cousin to me, he is my friend too. It was time to wake him up, so I gave him a great big kick, and out of the bed he flew! B-O-O-M!!, he hit the floor. He woke up quick when he hit the floor, and he looked up at me from where he landed.

"What in the sam hill did you do that for?" He asked.

I just started laughing.

"Okay, it is a little funny." He said as a big smile came across his face.

"So I'm up now and what have you got planned for us to do today?" He asked.

"Well the first thing we need to do is to get some food, but not waking up the whole house." I said. So we tiptoed into the kitchen and got some food out of the icebox. Then we wrote mom a note telling her that we were going down to see grandpa.

All the folk in Leeper Holler know my grandpa. And not just in Leeper, but in the whole county. They all know that old Charles Waist Laxton. He is the only moonshiner for 50 miles in any direction. And he has to work hard to stay up with the demand for it.

We decided to watch and follow grandpa back to his moonshine shed. We hid in the brush outside his house and watched for him to come out and head back into the woods. It was 7 a.m. and we sat there for 30 minutes watching his back door and eating our food. Finally we see the back door to his house open up, but we could not see who it was. A few seconds later we see my grandma come out and go to the chicken pen to get some eggs. And back into the house she went.

We knew the eggs were for grandpa to eat because he wouldn't eat anything that was not fresh. If it had been sitting on a store shelf, he didn't want it, he wouldn't even eat leftovers. We sat in the brush waiting about another 30 minutes. We were about to go out of our minds! Two young boys hiding, waiting, doing absolutely nothing but sitting quietly.

We were about ready to give up when the door finally opened and grandpa walked out. He had a big brown bag thrown up over one shoulter and a 12 gauge shotgun in the other hand. We knew he had used that shotgun before and even put people six foot under the ground, up beside the water tower. Much of the time, if he felt like someone was following him, he would just shoot over their head to scare them a little. Just to make them run away. The one he killed had found his moonshine still, and that was his livelihood! That was how he put food into his house, and no one messed with my grandpa's livelihood.

We followed from a good ways behind him so he could not see us. We went up and over one hill, two hills and three hills. We dropped off into the third big valley when grandpa began following a little creek up the valley. We followed that little creek right to its end where it seemed to be running right under the side of the hill.

There was grandpa's still right next to the spring. We stayed back in the woods hiding behind two trees and just watched him working around the still. I had heard a lot about this spring; it is supposed to have healing power, the one and only healing spring. Grandpa was working with his still, carrying water from the spring and putting it into the top of the still. Then he opened a little tap on the bottom of the still and some kind of liquid come from the tap.

I knew, even at age 10, that was moonshine in the jugs. He put four or five jugs into the big bag he had brought with him. Then he sat three beside the still and picked up his shotgun in one hand and the big bag in the other hand. As soon as he got them in his hands, down the valley he headed. We watched until he went out of our sight.

As soon as we were sure that grandpa was gone, we both came from behind the trees and headed to the still.

The second Junior got there he picked up a jug of shine and said, "Hey Mac. are we going to drink some?"

I looked at him and said "Does a bear poop in the woods?"

He looked at me with a crazy look on his face as if to say, "What!"

I said "Yes Junior, why would we follow grandpa here just to look at the still."

"Who is going first, you or me?" he asked.

I asked him if he had a penny so we could flip it and call heads or tails. Junior dug into his pockets and pulled out two pennies.

"We only need but one." I replied.

He gave me one of the pennies and I said, "Call it." as I threw it into the air. He called heads. I caught it in one hand placed it over the other hand, and then took my hand off and called out, "You got it, it's heads."

"I'm first." Junior said looking a little bit nervous. "But it doesn't matter what happens to me because after I drink it you still have to drink some, too."

I replied, "I will. Don't you worry 'bout it!"

"You're not going to do it, are you?" Junior asked me.

Junior was so nervous that I wasn't going to drink too that we decided to go together on the count of three. We opened two of the jugs that grandpa had set on the ground and counted slowly to three.. "Now here we go; one, two, three!" And up the jugs went to our lips. The moonshine poured into our mouths at right exactly the same time.

Oh God, it burned my mouth so much I wanted to scream and shout! When it made it's way to our throats it felt like we had swallowed a ball of fire! I didn't think it would feel as bad when it hit my belly. Boy was I wrong! the worst feeling was as it settled down to our bellies. I looked at Junior and his face was as red as a poker just out of a blazing fire. He had tears in his eyes, and I had never seen Junior cry anytime that I had been with him before. The second it hit my belly, I started to cough and gag.

"Junior, I think I'm dying." I managed to sputter.

"Me too." He said between his coughing and gagging.

We both got the idea at the same time, we ran and jumped into the cold water of the spring and started drinking the water as fast as we could. We found out real fast that this just made it worse. I heard someone laughing at us, so we turned and looked around, and we could see that it was grandpa!

He stopped laughing just long enough to say, "Now I'm going to have to kill you both." To my surprise, he pointed his shotgun right at me and said, "If I'm lucky maybe I can kill both of you with one shot."

I thought I was going crazy! My own grandpa was saying that he was going to shoot me, and hide my body somewhere it will never be found!

To my total surprise, Junior said, "Go head shoot me, put me out of my misery! If you don't kill me your moonshine will! But it will kill me slowly."

Grandpa turned the shotgun away from me and pointed it at Junior, and to my surprise, he pulled the trigger! I thought my heart had stopped for a second as Junior stumbled and fell back into the cold water of the spring. Grandpa started laughing again and said, "I'm not going to kill you, but you both got to promise not tell anyone where my still is. And no Christmas or birthday presents for you this year."

Junior looked a little funny and said, "But you don't get me any Christmas or birthday presents."

Grandpa replied, "I do now and here is $5 for each of you and I'll walk you boys back to town."

So he walked us to town and we bought so much candy we got sick and decided maybe moonshine and candy don't mix. Three days later we walked back to grandpa's still, but it was completely gone. I guess you never know someone as well as you think you do!

2

ELBOW ROOM

It was a cold October 29th, in 1961. Little Mac was waking up as he rolled out of bed and hit the floor with a thump. He was 8 years old and shared a bed with his sister Kathy, who could kick like a donkey in her sleep. It was about 6:00am. and he could hear his mother in the other room cooking some breakfast. So he got up off the floor and walked into the other room and sat down at the table. Little Mac had decided that it was time for him and Mom to have a talk about the sleeping arrangements.

He started by saying, "Mom I'm getting too big to be sleeping with my sister". His mom stopped cooking and looked at him, she realized that he was getting pretty big. "Ok," she said,

"Tonight you will start sleeping with your brother Dave."

My first thought was, 'Oh no, not Dave!' You have to understand that Dave is like the devil, and he has a way of making my life a living hell. He was the meanest kid in the whole world, no joke at all.

I cried, "Oh no Mom, not Dave. Kenny or Charles, but please not Dave."

She walked over to me bent down and kissed my forehead. With a smile she said, "You will be alright." But I had my doubts about that.

We all used to sleep in the same room, the whole family. Mom, dad, my sister, my three brothers and me in one little room. My mom thought about our conversation that morning and went to my dad. She told dad that she needed some elbow room, that it was just too many people in one room. So my dad had the bright idea that since he worked at the local sawmill he would bring home some of the scrap slabs and build us boys our own room.

Now let me tell you about that room that my dad built for us boys. It seemed like a great idea at the moment, but it turned out to be a real bad idea. Oh it was great until the bark fell off the slabs, and then the rain, snow, and wind would come right though the holes in the walls.

So dad got another clever idea, "I'll just get some cardboard boxes, flatten them out and put them over the holes in the wall."

Well that worked until the cardboard got wet, then it fell apart too. Dad had no more ideas on the matter, and the snow, rain and wind continued to blow through our bedroom. I only have three words to describe it. "IT WAS HELL". Only unlike hell, it was cold. We could not even leave a glass of water sitting out in our room, or else it would freeze solid.

It was hard but we grew up with a sincere respect for what we have now. And we learned not to look down on people who have nothing.

3

DOC HURLEY
AND THE JAMES GANG

It was half past five on Saturday morning. All the world was bright and brimming with life. Everyone was still asleep but me, little Mac. I'm heading out to go next door to see my old buddy, Doc Hurley. Doc Rode with the Jesse James Gang, or so he said. Old Doc was about ninety or so and no one knew for sure, but I loved that old man.

I got to Doc's door at the same time every Saturday. I knocked on the door and he said, "Come on in Mac. Pull up a seat and park your butt." So I came on in and sat down and old Doc began asking me things like, "Hey, little Mac, would you like a cup of good old moonshine?"

"Oh no Doc, just a cup of milk would do me fine." I would say. "How about some buttermilk biscuits with your milk?" He would holler with the door to his icebox open. Doc's biscuits were so hard that you could throw them at a rabbit and kill it!

But I always went home from Doc's with both of my pockets full of his homemade biscuits. So you know I said "Yes-sir-ee-bob!" to the biscuits. Old Doc got the milk and the biscuits and set them on the table beside me. Then he walked back to the old wood burning stove to get his. Now old Doc didn't like milk, and he kept it around just for me. He came back to the table with his biscuit and a cup of my grandpa's homemade moonshine. We would just sit and talk and sometimes he would tell me a story about when he rode with Jesse James. On this day, he told me how it came to be that he was called by the name of Doc. This is his story.

"It was September of 1872 and I was at the Kansas City Fair. There were a lot of people there and I was just another face in the crowd. I was about 13 year old, well I would be come December. It was later that afternoon when three men approached the ticket taker. I could see their guns were out so I walked a little closer to see what was going on. One of the men fired his gun at the ticket taker. The shot missed him, and hit a young girl in the leg.

They took the money from the ticket man and rode off. I found my horse and followed them but stayed a ways back so not to be seen. I followed them for about a day and then we entered Clay County. They headed up into a big holler. I knowed that I shouldn't have followed them into that holler but I did. Steep hills on both sides made it near impossible to go up with a horse. Only two ways to go, the way I was going, or to turn around and go back. So I just keep on going the way I was going up the holler. I rode right into a dead end, so now I could only turn and go back. I turned and headed back the way I came and thought I lost them.

I had just gone a little way further when I saw them, but they saw me too. I had no place to run, one of the men rode right up beside me with his gun pointing at me. He turned around and looked at the two men and shouted, "Hey, it's just a kid." Then he looked back at me and said, "I'm Jesse James, so who the sam hill are you, and why are you following us? Are you trying to get yourself killed?" I just looked at him at a total loss for words.

He said "Cat got your tongue, boy?"

I looked down at the ground and said, "I'd like to ride with you, I've got no home to go back to Mr. James."

" 'Mr', He said, "I like the sound of that!" Then he turned to the two men who were with him and said, "Hey, we could use a house boy to cook and clean couldn't we?" Jesse looked back at me and said, "Come on, but we all gonna be keeping an eye on you."

We rode about ten miles from the holler to a big cave, and we rode right up into it on the horses. About a half a mile back in the cave it seemed to really open up. A little house was sitting beside one wall of the cave. The man that didn't speak took our horses and we went inside the house.

Jesse said with a smile on his face "Here it is, home sweet home. Now get to work, I'm hungry!"

So I did just what he said, and cooked them a good meal. "Oh! I didn't tell you how I got the name Doc did I? See I used to help my dad on the farm to doctor up cows when they got hurt. One time a cow got shot and I had to help dad dig out the bullet. Well the boys would come in from a job all shot up sometimes and I got to doctoring Jesse's gang up. They begun calling me Doc and I liked the sound of it, so I just told everyone I met to call me Doc."

28

"Well, That's all of this story, but next Saturday I'll tell you how I ended up in Leeper Holler." So I said my goodbye. But I'll see him next week, if God is willing, for another Jesse James adventure.

Well my five days at school just seemed to fly by and I was in school just keep thinking about riding with the James gang. What fun it had to be for a kid, I bet it was so cool being there, Doc was so lucky. I went to sleep Friday night thinking and dreaming all about Jesse James, and the adventures they had. I woke up Saturday and couldn't wait to get to Doc's house.

I got to the door and knocked, and I could hear Doc on the inside cooking and singing some old song I never heard before. It was something about Jim Danny it sound like it come from the 1800's or something.

"Come on in Mac, sit down and take the weight off your feet." So I came on in and pushed up a bucket and sat down at the table. "Hey Mac would you like some milk and some biscuits? They're buttermilk biscuits!" Doc said with a big smile, like to say thanks for coming over and keeping a lonely old man company. He was standing at his old wood burning cooking stove with a cup of milk in one hand and in the other a plate of homemade biscuits. He sat them on the table in front of me and said, "Help yourself."

He turned back to the icebox to get a jug of moonshine out of it. He came back to the table with a jug of moonshine in one hand and a tin cup in the other hand. As he sat down he said, "Back to the story of how I ended up here in Leeper, Missouri. Well I'd been with the James gang about a year or maybe more, I was turning 14 years old.

Jesse came in and looked at me and said, "Doc, your almost a man now. How would like to go on a job with us?"

I replied, "I would love it, but I don't have a gun."

Jesse smile and said, "And you don't need one, you just a cook for us. It's goin' to be a three day trip. We all goin' to go down south to a little town called Gasp Hills and goin' to camp out at the Black River. That camp is about 15 mile from the job and that's the closest you are goin' to get to the job."

"Come on Jesse give me a break I'm almost a man, you just said it yourself." I explained. All the men were sittin around the table just to watch us argue.

Cole Younger said "He got you there Jesse." And all the men began to laugh. Jesse said "Alright kid you asked for it. We will all go to the Black River to make camp. Doc you're not wanted anywhere so as we are making camp you can go to a little town called Leeper and get food for four days."

So we packed everything we could carry on our horses, and rode out going south. It took three days of hard riding to get to our campsite on the great Black River.

When we got to the campsite Jesse said to me, "Ride back to the train tracks we passed a little bit ago, and go south along them for a mile 'til you come to Leeper."

So I just got on my horse a headed on over to town to get food for us. It took me about one hour, and by the time I got back, they had already made camp. As I rode up Jesse took a 30 minute break and then got our horses unloaded and I started cooking. We all ate and got ourselves to bed. Tomorrow was going to be a big day, it was Doc's first job. Everyone was asleep quick except for the lookout.

The next day we were up before the sun. Jesse told Cole Younger "We need someone to watch the camp. And shut your mouth about Doc going with us. It's going to be your job to watch the camp, maybe you will keep you mouth closed next time." Cole didn't say anything, he just threw a piece of wood at the ground a walked away. The rest of us got our horses ready to go.

Jesse told Cole that we should be back five or six hours. If not, then close up camp and head back home.

Cole simply replied, "Ok."

With that we rode off. In two hours we got to Gasp Hills, then we rode about five minutes south on the railroad tracks. Where we stopped, there was a big hill each side of the track. Jesse told everyone what to do.

My job was to get on one side of the track and roll some big rocks down onto the tracks. And then wait there as they got on the train then they would wave at me when they came back out of the train. Everything had to be perfect, the train had shipment of gold on it.

Soon after we got ready I heard the train whistle blowing. I rolled the big rocks on to the track as Jesse had told me to. The train was coming up the track fast! The man who was driving saw the rocks on the track, so he put the brake on. The train stopped about a foot from the rocks, some workers jumped out of the front of the train and as they jumped out, Jesse and the boys jumped on to the back of the train.

I could see it all clear from where I was sitting. The men from the train started moving the rocks from the train track. It took ten minutes to get the track cleared and the men headed back to the train.

32

I keep looking for Jesse and the boys to get off the train but they hadn't. I thought to myself hurry up Jesse. The train was starting to move again. About that time, jumping off the train with bags in his hands was Jesse and the boys with four more brown bags.

Jesse waved at me to get on my horse and ride down the back side of the hill and meet them at the bottom of it. By the time I got down the hill, I saw Jesse and the boys waiting for me already on the horses. We rode off as Jesse said, "Good job! When a shots not fired at all, it's a great job!" We rode back to our camp on Black River. When we rode up, Cole said, "You all are back in four hours, good job."

I got off my horse and started cooking. It had been a long day and we were all hungry. After we ate, Jesse again told all of us, "Good job men, but we got a long way to go to get back home." I was thinking that we need to hide the gold somewhere before we ride on home. So I told the guys what was on my mind. "There is going to be a lot of lawmen looking for this gold. I was thinking that we were better off without it. Especially if we got stopped along the way home." "Maybe we should hide it." Jesse suggested. We all said okay, but that Jesse should be the one to hide it. So Jesse took one load and headed into the woods, that was the first of four trips. It took about ten minutes every time, so it had to be pretty close to our camp. After that we all just sat around and took it easy.

A little later Cole was cleaning his gun, and it went off hitting me right in the shoulder. The bullet went in the front and out the back of my shoulder.

Jesse cried out, "Oh God Cole, you are such a dummy."

I was bleeding bad. Frank got a clean rag and wrap my shoulder up. "Jesse," Frank said, "What are we going to do?"

Jesse said "Let me think....I got it. Doc, you know the little place where you got the food from?" I replied "Yes!"

"Cole will ride with you to that town because he is the dummy that got you hurt. You can just stay in Leeper and when we come back to get the gold we will get you."

So we said goodbye, then me and Cole took off. The pain was the worst I had ever had in my life. The 15 minute ride seemed like a lifetime.

When we got to the doctor's house and Cole said, "I can't go in with you because I'm wanted by the law, I've got a poster on me."

I said, "Okay". He told me how sorry he was and he hoped things would go well for me. With that he rode off. I told the doctor I had a hunting accident. He took it at that and took me in, and cared for me like his own son for three years. I worked hard, and when I was 18 I got this house, but I never saw Jesse again. I heard that he went to his house, to his wife and kids, and got shot and killed by one of his own men.

I looked for that gold all my life. I dug over 10,000 holes in the woods near the campsite we had so many years ago. I never to this day found that gold. It's still up there waiting for someone to find it. Now you know how I got to this town of Leeper, Missouri.

I do not know how many you had hurt: I do know how happy you made a lonely boy. How you charged his life with your stories, how you made him love you with his whole heart! Rest easy and may God open His doors for this old man that helped a boy to grow into a good man.

-Love you Doc!

4

THE JOKE
THAT KILLED

It is 1963, I'm 10 years old. It's a cold and snowy afternoon in a southern town in the backwoods of Missouri. A little boy is out playing with friends on the snowy hillside. I'm the boy that they call Little Mac. The other boys I'm playing with are my cousin Junior who had spent the night with me, and two other boys are named Ricky and Cecil. Ricky and Cecil are both a big bully and a joker.

We were sledding on the biggest hill in Leeper Holler. Every time we would slide down the hill we would end up right in blind John's front yard. John is an old blind man who lives by himself, he would often ask the kids of Leeper Holler to run to town for him. John had heard us playing outside and was waiting for the next boy to come down the hill.

So as Ricky slid down the hill and into John's front yard, John called out to Ricky, "Hey would you go to town for me? I'll pay you."

Ricky ran over to talk to John, now we could not hear what they were saying, but we saw Ricky go to the side of the house and pick up a five gallon can. A minute or two later Ricky came walking up the hill to where we were all standing at the top.

He said to us, "John asked me to run to town for him and get him some kerosene so that he can get his fire started tonight. And he gave me a whole dollar to do it."

Cecil said, "I got a great joke we can play on old John."

"What?" Said Ricky. Junior and I just stood there listening as Cecil was explaining the joke to us. "We go to town and fill his kerosene can full of gasoline and when he tries to start his fire tonight the gas will explode at him."

"That will scare the old mad to death. Is that going to be funny?" I asked.

Ricky said, "That will be funny!"

I said, "I don't think it's a good idea, he could get hurt or something."

As I was objecting, Ricky walked up behind me and grabbed both of my arms and pulled them behind my back. Cecil walked over to me and hit me right in the nose and said, "If you babies tell anyone about our plan we will give you both some more of this." My nose was bleeding pretty bad, so I got handful of snow and put it on my nose in hopes of stopping the bleeding. Junior asked me if I was alright? I told him that I would be fine.

Junior and I got our sleds and left because we didn't want any part of those plans. On the way home we were talking about how many ways their plan could go wrong and someone could get hurt. I asked Junior, "Do you think we should tell someone?"

Junior replied about as fast as I said it, "No way! They can and will hurt us bad. They were not playing about beating us up. No way, no, I am not telling anyone."

I was so angry by his answer. By the time we got to my house it was time to eat, and after we ate it was too late to go back out and play. So we sat around playing games until it was time to go to bed at 9:00 pm. My three brothers had the bed taken up that night, so Junior and I decided to make a bed in the living room. But that was cool with us because Dave had his friend staying the night. Dave and his friend were two of the meanest boys you have ever seen. So we needed to stay as far away from them as we could.

We didn't go right to bed. We fixed up a cot on the floor and then told some jokes. We were laughing so loud that mom and dad had to tell us to be quiet around ten. After that we decided that maybe it was time to get some sleep.

Around midnight, Junior and I woke up to someone hammering loud on the front door. We were the first ones awake because we were on the floor in the front room. I got up quick to see who it was and was surprised to find Ricky's dad there.

He asked me to go get my dad up as fast as I could. So I ran into the other room to get mom and dad. I told them that he was at the door wanting them to come right away. I followed my dad to the door so that I could listen to them talk.

He told my dad, "Blind John's house is on fire and he is still in it. We could hear him calling out for help."

Dad ran into his bedroom to get some clothes on quick. So I told Junior that we ought to get dressed and go check it out. We got going as fast as we could and followed dad up the road to John's house.

By the time we got there the house was totally engulfed by the fire. Junior hit me on the shoulder as he saw Ricky and Cecil coming our way.

"Oh no. It's time for us to go back home now." But it was too late, they were already following us. I slowed down and let them catch up with us because I had something I had to say to those two jokers.

Before they could say a word I got in Ricky's face and told him, "You know that if John got burned up in that fire it is your fault. You two are the reason this happened."

Cecil said "The old man did burn up, and me and Ricky don't care, not even a little bit. We killed John and if you boys tell even one person, just one, we will get you and douse you in gas and burn you up just like we did him!"

Junior and I knew that they would, because they were both was as crazy as bed bug. So blind John died that night and nobody knew the truth until now. It's too late to get justice for John but it not too late to get it out of my head.

When a joke hurts someone, that is when the joke stops being funny!
-John this is for you!

LEGENDS OF LEEPER HOLLER

5

THE
NIPPER WOODS
BIGFOOT

I got up before any of my family was awake and I tip-e-toed through the house. I looked at my three brothers sleeping and was thinking to myself what I could do to get back at Dave. Dave was one of my older brothers who had made it his life's mission to make me miserable.

There's a nasty mud hole out back in the pig pen. So I walked out back and got a handful of mud and tip-e-toed back into the house. I walked past my mom and dad sleeping, and my sister Kathy. I walked back into my brother's room with some stinky mud in one hand and holding my nose with the other. Dave always slept in his under pants so his pants were lying by his bed. I picked up the pants as quiet as I could and filled one leg full of the mud and sneaked back out of the house. I was headed next door to my good friend Doc Hurley's house.

Old Doc was about 90, and was the town drunk. But I loved the old man, he was a good friend to a lonely 10 year boy. As I walked into his house he was cooking on an old wood stove. He said, "Hey little Mac, would you like something to eat? Pull up a bucket and sit down." Doc didn't have any chairs just some old buckets to sit on.

So I pulled up a bucket and sat down. Doc asked what was going on so I told him about what I had done to Dave and we both had a good laugh about it. He sat down a plate of bacon and eggs, with a biscuit on the side. His biscuits were so hard you could kill a rabbit with them, so I stuck the biscuit in my pocket rather than eating it.

As we started eating, someone knocked at the front door. His house was a shotgun home, which means you walk in the front door and arrive at the back door in just a few steps. So Doc got up and headed for the front door. I could hear him call out to ask who was there, then he said, "It's not locked, come on in and stop the darn knocking before you wake the whole town up!" He got to the front door at the same time it flew open and hit him right in the head. As he shook his head and let out some bad words, I tried to stifle my laughter and heard him say, "Oh it's you!" It was Tuffy.

Tuffy was an old one-armed man that lived up at the edge of Leeper. He was a wino and the people didn't like him much.
They would go the other way so they wouldn't have to see or talk to him. But he was my friend and I loved to hear him tell his stories. He was a great storyteller, especially about ghosts and other unearthly terrors in the dark.

One thing about Tuffy, he was always in a hurry. He came running into Doc's house talking fast like he always did. Asking if me and Doc would go pick some blackberries with him. See Tuffy was wanting to make a blackberry cobbler and that sounded just fine to Doc, so he said that was a good idea. Then he said, "Little Mac would like to go along with us?" I told him that I would have to go and ask my mom. Tuffy told me I had better make it fast because he was wantin' to get going.

I started out the door then turned back and asked where we were going to pick blackberries at. Tuffy said we were going to the nipper woods. As I got to the back door of my house I could hear mom cooking inside. I was trying to think of how I could word my question so she would let me go with them.

I thought I had it, so in I went. After I gave my mom a kiss and said good morning I jumped right in… "Mom, them crazy old men are going into the nipper woods to look for blackberries, and I know if them two men go by themselves they could get hurt bad. They need me to go just to keep an eye on them!" The moment I looked into her eyes I knew she wasn't buying my story.

She said, "Little Mac go tell Tuffy and Doc it would be a cold day in hell before I let my 10 year old boy go with them across the street much less five miles to the nipper woods to spend the day alone with them. Have I got stupid written across my forehead?!?!"

So with my head hanging down, I went next door to Doc's house and with a sad tone in my voice said "Sorry guys I can't go, Mom's got work for me to do today." Tuffy and Doc were sorry that I couldn't go, since they could have used the extra hands. They were really anxious to get started so they would be able to make it back before dark. They grabbed a couple of buckets and were on their way, without me. And I headed home.

All day long I kept on thinking about how much fun Doc and Tuffy must be having without me. The day drug on and I could hardly wait to talk to Tuffy and Doc to see how their day was. It was getting dark and still no word from them. I was getting worried. I walked around and sat on the front porch. I stared down the road and tried to see through the darkness. The road was as silent as a graveyard.

Then I heard someone talking and I could tell by the voice that it was Tuffy! I could see Tuffy in front and Doc was lagging behind. Tuffy's shirt was torn and hanging off of him in shreds. Doc was as white as a ghost. Tuffy was talking a lot but Doc was not saying a word. As they got closer to me I asked what had happened? Tuffy murmured, "It was not a ghost, it was something else."

He told me to walk over to Doc's and have a seat on the porch so he could tell me all about it. As we sat down he began talking about the strange happenings of the day. When they arrived at the nipper woods they found a big old blackberry path and begun picking blackberries as fast as their hands could go.

They didn't even stop to take a drink of wine. Right about the time they had the bucket almost full of berries they heard something heading down the hill! Each step made the ground shake, so they sat down to take a better look around. Berries were toppling from the bucket as the ground shook.

Doc said "Tuffy! Let's get behind that big tree there!"

So they hid behind the tree and when they sneaked a peek out from behind the tree, they saw it.

"What did you see, what was it?" I asked.

"It was as big as a mountain, and it had more hair on it's body than my ex-girlfriend had on her, and she had hair everywhere. She could even grow a better beard than I could." Tuffy said.

Still Doc hadn't said a word, not one word! Tuffy just kept talking. He said as it got closer, we could see it was a Bigfoot! It got to the blackberry path and saw there was no blackberries left on the bush. It walk over where the berries had fell from our bucket and picked them up off the ground and ate them right down. It looked right at us like the tree was not there at all.

It let out a growl that shook the hat right off of my head. Doc got real scared, and threw his whole bucket of berries down at the Bigfoot's feet. The Bigfoot was not happy just having Doc's berries, he came right up to me and growled in my face so hard my fake teeth fell out of my mouth on to the ground!

As I stood there toothless I thought to myself, if I don't give him my berries he is going to get me. So I threw my berries at his feet and he sat down on the ground to eat my berries I had worked so hard for. I took off as fast as I could only looking for a second to see what Doc was doing.

He was standing there like a frozen man, and as white as one too. But I kept running as fast as I could through the berry path. The thorns were pulling at my shirt and tearing it to threads! As I got on the other side of the berry path, I was running so fast I couldn't slow down for the big hill and I fell head over heels as I got the bottom of the hill.

I came to rest as my head hit a big rock knocking me out. A little later I woke up thinking, where my buddy Doc was at. The last time I saw him he was at the tree face to face with Bigfoot. So I got up and ran back to the top of the hill and headed in the berry path again. I got to the other side of the berry path. I could see Doc still standing in the same place with the same look on his face, and not moving at all.

I tried to talk to him, but he would not move at all. And he is still not talking. I looked at Doc and Tuffy and I said, "I've got it, just wait here I'll be right back."

I ran into Doc's house and got his moonshine out and poured a cup of it and headed back off to see Doc and Tuffy on the porch. I told Tuffy, "With your good arm hold his top lip up."

49

With one hand I held the cup of moonshine, with the other I pried his mouth open. As he opened up I poured his mouth full of the moonshine. As he swallowed the shine he began to wake up and get his color back. He said "Tuffy are we going to go and pick some blackberries or not?"

Tuffy said "We did go!"

Doc said "Have you gone crazy? We have not gone to get berries!"

We told him the whole story but he never remembered it. Like it hadn't happened at all.

6

THE FIRST DAY
OF SCHOOL

It is 1959 and I am a 6-year-old boy. It's the first day of school and I'm so excited! I can't wait to make some new friends. Leeper Holler is so small...like 10 kids in the whole holler, and half of them are family. We have to be at school by 7 a.m so we have to get up at 4:30 a.m. We have to do our chores before we can get dressed in our school clothes.

Today is my brother Dave's turn to feed the pigs but he said it's not his turn. My big brother Charles could do it, but he works. Mom and Dad said he has a car and a girlfriend, he has to work for the money for them. Oh..I almost forgot to tell you my job. I had to feed and water the rabbits, a great job today.

By the time we all get done with our work –
the pigs and the chickens and rabbits and fetching
the water, Mom would have breakfast on the table,
so we could all eat together. As soon as we finish
eating, it is time to get dressed for school. I just
could not wait to get to school and make new
friends!

By this time it was getting close to 6 a.m.
To get to school it took about 45 minutes to walk
there. Mom would have our bag lunches sitting on
the table waiting for us. It didn't matter which one
you took because they all were the same - we all
had a peanut butter sandwich and a jug of water.

We all grabbed our lunches and headed
down the road for the long walk to school. Mom
stopped me for just a minute and told me, "You
have new clothes on, not hand-me-downs, so try
not to get them in a mess."

"Okay." I said. And was thinking if I can
stay away from my brother Dave I will be able to
stay clean. I walked with my sister, Kathy, so I
don't have to deal with him right now. Kathy and I
were walking ahead because Dave had to go up the
holler from our house to get his friend, little boy.
That was the only name I knew him by. He was
about as bad as Dave, but then no one could be
THAT bad.

Suddenly, I feel a big hard hit to the back of my head. It had to be Dave and that little boy behind us. 'I'm going to get it now', I thought. Dave yelled at me because I was with the girls, "I knew you were a girl. I bet you have sit to pee, don't you little girl." He hit me on the head again; I thought I saw stars this time. About that time, Tom ran by and I said to my sister, good! because I knew there was one person in town Dave and 'little boy' loved picking on more than me, and it was Tom.

They took off after him. "Thank God." I said to myself. Maybe I can get to school with out getting beaten-up. We walked about a half a mile farther and I saw Dave and little boy by a well and Tom was naked as a jaybird. Dave and little boy had taken Tom's clothes off and put them in the well. Tom was crying, holding his hands over his boy parts. I felt sorry for him but was not going to say anything about it, or my new clothes would be in the well too. I just walked on with Kathy and got myself to school. Glad that I was still wearing clean clothes for now.

I stayed in school and didn't go outside to play at recess time with all the other kids because I don't want to run into Dave outside. I could just think of all the things he could do to me out there, and thought, "No thanks. I'll just stay in here where it is safe."

It was lunch time and we all ate our lunches. Dave is as crazy as a bedbug, but not crazy enough to do something in the school. Right after lunch I needed to go to the outdoor bathroom. I was thinking to myself, maybe I can hold it because it's just three hours more. The first 10 minutes were not bad, but it was beginning to stink like a polecat had gotten into the schoolhouse. I lifted my hand and told Miss Read, our teacher, that I had to go. She was the teacher for all six grades so she had no time to go with me. She told my cousin, Junior, "Your cousin, Little Mac, needs to go the bathroom so please go with him." Junior asked, "Why?" with a funny look on his face. Miss Read said, "Because he is new here and I said TO!"

"Okay," Junior said. But you could tell by the look on his face he was not happy. We walked out of the classroom and entered a long hall way. As we walk down the hall Junior said, "Nothing against you, but your crazy brother Dave is at recess now. You know how he is!" I looked at him and said, "Yes, I'm sorry to say I do!"

We got to the doors of the school. We looked out the glass of the doors looking for Dave or 'little boy'. We couldn't see them anywhere, but we knew that they were around somewhere. So we headed outside, we walked slowly and looked around like we were looking out for a pack of wolves in the grass. We got to the bathroom alright but I told Junior, "Stand watch in case my brother shows up."

I went in to do my business, but after about a second or two Junior was knocking at the door and crying "Let me in. I'm not going stay out here and let Dave kill me." I opened the door and let him in, "Hurry up before he gets here!" he said with a sad look on his face. Just then we heard a noise outside the door. It was Dave and little boy, we were both so scared. We heard him locking the door from the outside. He said, "Hey little girls, we will see you after school and then we heard a laugh.

I got finished as quick as I could and tried running into the door to break the lock off but it didn't work. Junior put his head in his hands and said, "I just knew something like this would happen."

I said, "Let me think a second, just a second. Okay, I've got it!" I said.

"What have you got, just what have you got?" Junior asked with a cry. I said, "We can crawl down though the toilet hole to the big hole in the back of the outhouse. But, we will have to take off our clothes because if I get my clothes dirty I'm dead."

He finally agreed, "Okay." We took off our clothes and began to slide down the dark hole looking for light in the back of the cistern.

Slow and easy, step-by-step we went down. One wrong step and we would be up to our knees in poo and would smell like polecats. Junior cried out, "There is a wasps nest in here." About that time, one got on him and he fell on me and I fell into the poo, with Junior right on top of me.

We crawled out of the back with poo on every inch of our naked bodies. We both ran around to the front to get our clothes but the door was open and our clothes were gone. We heard Dave laughing so we looked to where the laughter was coming from. We saw Dave and 'little boy' with our clothes in their hands.

"Hey look at this," Dave said, as they tossed our clothes on top the school roof as we both cried "NO." There we were, naked and covered with poo from our heads to our toes! All I could think about was what Mom was going to do to me if my clothes got torn up, but right now I'm going have to think about walking by all the kids on the playground and then walking into the classroom with poo all over our naked... "Let's get this over with." I cried.

We began walking by the kids on the playground. Little Sue was the first one to see us. She cried out to all the other kids, "Look at Little Mac. And, Junior is naked, too."

They all looked around at us laughing and pointing. We walked as fast as we could to get into the school, as fast as possible! We made it to the long hallway, and it seemed like an hour to walk that hallway with the kids outside fighting to look into glass doors to see our nude butts. We finally got to the classroom, a trip that seemed like a lifetime. As we walked into the classroom, all the kids heads turned our way as they began laughing and pointing at us. We hung our heads and thought we were going to be dead. At that time, Miss Read turned around from the blackboard and I though her eyes were going to hit the floor.

She started crying, "No-no-no, in the hallway now!" We headed back to the hallway and all the kids were still looking through the glass in the doors. When Miss R. got to the hallway, she saw the kids looking though the windows and ran them off. "Now," she said, "What is going on?"

We both just said not a word! She said, "Okay Junior, you are the oldest so start talking now." He finally told her the story and I just nodded my head to say that was the way it happened. Miss Read said, "Okay, we got to get you boys cleaned up and your clothes off the roof."

After we got all that done, she looked at us with a smile on her face. "Now it's time for Dave and 'little boy' to get their just dues."

I didn't like sound of that because what ever is done to him, he was going to give it back to me three times over. When school was out I had not made any new friends, but I did get a song made up about me and I didn't like it at all.

On the good side of it, my new clothes didn't get dirty.

That was Little Mac's first day of school. How was yours?

7

THE BOY
ON ALL FOURS

My great uncle Ben owned a bar that sat on the biggest hill in Leeper, overlooking the whole town. Ben use to say, "This bar is my throne, and the whole town around it is my foot stool." He was a good man, but just a little bit crazy. All the people of Leeper loved him and would have trusted him with their life. Until it happened and it drove him mad, and he had to be put away in the crazy house.

Well let me tell you the story. It was a cold December evening, two days before Christmas. As snow was falling on the sleepy little town, Ben was getting ready to close the bar for the night. He got all the money he made that day, and he put it in a brown bag and locked up the bar. Walking to his old car he was nearly shivering in the wind. Only three people in Leeper owned a car, and he was one of them.. As he got to the car he looked at the road and was thinking it's a lot of snow to try to drive down that big hill.

He got in anyway because it was too cold to walk home. He started up the car, and hadn't hardly gone anywhere when the car slid off into the ditch. It plowed right into a tree, and he hit his head hard on the windshield.

A big ole knot was already coming up on his head. Ben got out of the car and looked at it for a minute shaking his head. "I guess I'm going to have to walk home." Ben told himself. It was only about a mile if he take the short cut though the flat woods. So he got his money and a flashlight, and headed off to his house. About the middle of the big hill, he shone his light into the woods looking for a tiny path that ran straight though the flat woods to Leeper holler.

A smile came across his face, thinking about the stories people told about the flat woods. But he knew people didn't walk in the flat woods at night, and it would save him a mile. So down the narrow, dark, spooky pathway he went. His flashlight in one hand and a bag of money in the other, Ben also had his .38 in the bag with the money.

After he got just a few minutes into the woods, he heard something behind him. Ben turned to get a looks at whatever was following him. He saw something, but he thought it was just the darkness playing tricks on him. So he turned around and started walking again with the noises still back behind him. He started walking faster and whatever that was behind him started waking faster too.

Ben took his .38 from the bag and turned around suddenly. There it was! It was a boy about 18 years old and he was on all fours, with only had a rag covering his private parts up. His hair was as black as the dark night. His eyes were shining in the dark as the flashlight hit them, they were wild looking, like wolf eyes!

Ben said with a puzzled look on his face, "I don't know what you think you going to get, but I know what I'm going to give you, if you don't turn around a go away RIGHT NOW!" The boy just looked at Ben and moved his head from side to side as if to say, "I don't understand what you are saying to me.'

Ben didn't care, he was cold and just needed to get home with his bag of money. So he turned around and started walkin away from the boy, because he didn't want to have to shoot a kid. He began to run on the path to just get home. The boy began running too. Ben had finally had enough. He stopped and turned around, he shot him three times and the boy fell and rolled a little down the hill.

Ben said to his self "I got him; I'll come back and check up on him tomorrow." With that he turned and again started walking home. but in less than five minutes, he heard something let out a howl! Then there was more howling. There was three, four, or maybe five wolves! He turned around to see. It was the boy leading a pack of wolves and they looked vicious, growling and showing their teeth, and they were coming right after him. "Oh God what have I done?" He thought out loud.

So he turned and ran as fast as his legs would carry him. He knew they were getting closer to him, but he did not turn around again, he just kelp running. He came off the path into Leeper Holler, and the first place he saw was Doc's house. So he ran up and started hammering on the door. He could still hear the boy and the wolves coming through the woods.

He was thinking, 'If I don't get in that house they are going to kill me. If I just walk in, Doc could shoot me, he could shoot me but the boy and them wolves are going to kill me, I just know it.' So with that he opened the door, and ran into the house. He closed the door behind him, and locked it as fast as he could!

By this time old Doc had got up with his shotgun in his hands. "What the cotton pickins going on here?" Doc said, with a mad look across his face. By that time the boy and the wolves were at his house, and were biting and scratching at the door, trying to get in. Old Doc smiled and said "Friends of yours Ben?"

Ben said "Not any friends of mine Doc!"

Ben told Doc the story about the boy on his all fours but Doc wasn't buying it. Until he looked out the window in the back room and saw the wolves at the back door. Doc said "Well Ben, your right, there is a boy with them wolves. And I thought I'd seen everything!" They stayed there just about all night trying to get in, but had no luck.

Doc and Ben just sat there drinking my grandpa's homemade moonshine until they passed out. They both told the story over and over but everyone thought it just the moonshine talking. One night in March the town mayor was taking a walk along the flat wood paths and came back to town with his clothes just a hanging off him and ripped to pieces, like a pack of wolves had got a hold of him.

He told the same story Doc and Ben had told about a boy on his all fours. With a little checking, we found out about 17 years before that some people were camped out in the flat woods, and a one year old baby had crawled away from the camp and was never found. The men of town went back in the flat wood looking at day,(because no one would go in the dark of night) but with no luck. I bet he is till out there running with the wolves even to this day.

8

BURNT ENDS

I woke up to the sun shining in my eyes. Mom had hung an old rug over the window in the front room, but all the holes dinnit do much to stop the sunlight coming in. I looked over to the floor at my cousin Junior who was still sleeping. He had stayed overnight with me, and we got to stay up into the wee hours.

I got up as quiet as I could and tip-e-toed into the kitchen. I saw the bucket of water that my brother Kenny had drawn from the town well before he went to work. Kenny had to get up before the sun so he could get his chores done before he went to work.

I got an idea, cold water would wake Junior up and it would be funny too. So I got a glass of water and tip-e-toed back to the front room and looked down at Junior sleeping on the floor. I thought to myself how can I do this. I could just throw it on his face, not funny enough. I could throw it on his pants, but he would be mad because he only had one pair of pants with him. Then I got it! I would put it in his hand, and go out and get a chicken feather from the chicken pen.

I put the water in his hand and I got up quiet and tip-e-toed out the front door. Thinking all the way to chicken pen that this is going to be so funny. I got the feather and ran to the front door, I quietly opened the door and tip-e-toed back into the house. I got on my knees in front of Junior's head and started moving the feather under his nose. He began moving his nose a little. I almost let out a big laugh, but I held my breath to stop it from coming out.

Just a couple more tickles I thought! So I twitched the feather under his nose again. He jerked the water in his hand, and threw it right in my face! As fast as it hit me in my face, he let out a big laugh.

"No fun!" I said, "No fun at all!"

"It was funny little Mac." He giggled, "Because your plan backfired on you!"

I looked at him with a loser look on my face and said "You was playing poses on me the whole time." He looked at me with a look of a winner on his face and said, "Yeps."

"It was a little bit fun." I said with a half smile across my face. I headed to the kitchen to get a rag to wash off my face. Junior followed right behind me talking about being hungry. I told him "You know we are not allowed to get into the food without asking Mom."

She was still sleeping. "Do you what to wake her up? because I know I don't!"

It was the weekend, the only two days she got to sleep in. We needed to find something to do, to take our minds off of eating. Junior looked at me with a half grin on his face. I knew that grin meant trouble for me, and in my house when you got in trouble, it was bad.

So I looked at him with a worried look on my face and asked, "What?"

He said "You know your brother Charles?"

I replied "Yes, I know Charles dummy, he is my brother."

Junior said "Well I saw him hide his smokes last night when he came home from his date." I knew he was telling the truth, because in my house if you get caught smoking, you were in for it. And it didn't matter how old you were.

Charles was 19 and he still knew better than to bring smokes into mom's house.

I said "Ok, so what?"

Junior said "There some matches in the kitchen and I know where some smokes is. Put two and two together little Mac!"

I thought to myself, I can count and it still adds up to trouble for me. I never tried the smokes before, so I let curiosity take over my good sense. I said "Ok! Let's go for it!" So we headed to the kitchen to get the matches. As soon as we got the matches, we tip-e-toed outside.

Junior followed me, and we went out to the back of the house. He said "Down there!" Pointing to the root cellar!

I said "Okay, but don't break any of my mom's can goods. We started down the dark stairs to the cellar door. We slowly opened the door and it was dark as night in there.

Junior lit a match so we could see our way. We got to the back of the cellar and he pointed up at an air pipe in the cellar roof. So I put up a bucket lying on the floor under the pipe. As Junior held the matches in his hand, I climbed up on the bucket and put my hand in the pipe.

As I felt around in the pipe, I thought about a snake taking a bite out of my hand, or maybe a spider. It only took a second and I felt the smokes.

I grabbed them and said "Let's get the heck out of here!". So we got out of the cellar as fast as we could.

"Now, where can we go to hide and try one?" Junior asked.

I looked at him and said "The front porch!"

"A great place to hide, little Mac, a great place!" Junior said. So we ran out and got on our knees and crawled back under the porch. We got as far as we could go and stopped. Junior told me "I've tried smokes before, and since you haven't, you can go first.

"I'm only nine and you're only ten, so how could you have tried them before?" I asked.

"At school, big John made me! It was I try a smoke, or he was going to beat me up, so I tried the smoke.

I took one out of the pack and put it between my lips, it tasted bad.

Junior had the matches in his hands, he took one out and lit it. Junior told me, "Suck as hard as you can on the smoke as soon as I get the match to the end of the smoke, okay?"

I said "Okay!" And as soon as he got the match to the end of the smoke, I sucked super hard.

As I sucked on the cigarette, the flame from the match got bigger. It got so big it flared up and caught the ends of my hair on fire! I got so much of the smoke down my throat I began coughing and could not stop! Junior started patting my hair, trying to get the fire off.

By the time I stopped coughing and he got my hair put out, My hair was burnt so bad on the end! I began crying out "Oh no! Mom is gonna kill me, she is going to beat me till I'm dead!

Junior cried out "I've got an idea!"

I replied "Junior, your ideas got me in this condition in the first place!"

"Are you going listen to me or what?"

I said. "I guess I will, just because I've got none."

"Okay" he said. Let's go to the town well and draw some water." "We are not allowed at the well though, if we get caught, then we are gonna make the whole town mad at us!"

"I'm all ears if you can think of something we can do." Junior said.

"Okay." I replied. But I was scared we were going to get caught. We slowly crawled out from under the porch and made our way up the road to the well.

We looked around to see if anyone was in sight. Junior said "All the town folk are still sleeping!" So we walked up to the right side the well where the bucket was. As I slowly dropped the bucket into the well, Junior kept a lookout.

I dropped the bucket into the water and filled it full of water. Then I put the rope on the bucket till it was back to the top. I looked at Junior and said "Now what?"

He said "Put some water on your hands and wet your hair down with the water."

So I did as he said. "What now?" I asked.

He just reached into his back pocket and pulled out a comb. "Now comb your hair back." I did as he said.

"Let me see." Junior said.

"It looks great, no burnt ends Little Mac."

I asked "What about when it dries?"

"Little Mac, we can think on that went it happens." Junior replied.

By that time mom was calling out the back door, "Little Mac, Junior it's time to eat!" So we hurried back to my house. As we walked into the back door mom looked hard at my hair. "Hey little Mac, You are looking good! If you weren't my son I would give all the little girls around here a fight for you."

My brother Dave was sitting at the table, and I knew he wouldn't be quiet about me. So he said "He looks like a big geek!"

Mom told him to be quiet, and for us to go wash our hands. We did as we were told and by the time we got back, the whole family was sitting around the table.

So we took our seat, mom blessed the food, and we all started eating. In the middle of eating my hair was getting dry, and one piece at a time started falling down. I was not paying attention. Junior whispered in my ear, "Your hair!"

"Oh Mom, I need to go to the bathroom?" I blurted out.

On that she replied, "You can wait until we all get done eating."

By this time my hair had all fallen down. I thought maybe she wouldn't notice.

My brother Dave was looking at me so hard it was like he was looking right though me. "Hey Mom!" Dave said. "The little geek has burnt the end of his hair off!"

Mom looked right at me and jumped up from her chair! She ran around like the house was on fire. She got right up in my face and she started staring at my hair. She made me open my mouth so she could smell my breath, and my clothes. She said with a mad look on her face, "Boys get up and go out back and get me a switch!"

As we were leaving, Dave said "The little geek is in trouble now! Ha! Ha!"

74

Mom looked right at him and asked, "Do you need some too?"

"No." He replied.

So I get in the back yard looking for a switch. I knew it needed to be a thin one, and a long one. Because I had been here before, I'm not the new kid when it comes to picking a switch. We waited by the root cellar for her. I could tell Junior was scared about being switched. I knew its going to hurt, but just for a day or two.

We saw the back door come open, and Mom walked out. I could tell by the way she was walking she was really mad. "Where did you get the smokes from?"

I wanted to speak up first, because Junior would spill the beans about how we found them. And I knew my brother Charles would hurt me ten times more than Mom would!

"Where did you boys find them at?" She asked again.

Junior opened his mouth first. "The pack was over by the well, and I put them back where we found them."

I thought, 'Oh no, now we are in trouble for smoking, and being by the well! You big dummy!'

Mom looked at Junior and said, "Go get them now!" So he went.   "LITTLE MAC! Let us see, you're in trouble for playing with fire, smoking and for being by the well. Did I leave anything else out?" Mom asked.

"No Mom, you got everything." I said. Before dummy Junior could get back and think of something else. After a minute or so, Junior had made it back with the smokes and the matches, and gave them to her. "Oh!" she said. "You took my matches from the kitchen! Something else I can add to the list."

"Alright little Mac, push your pant legs up." Mom said. So I did as I was told and she lay into my legs with the switch. It felt like fire burning me every time that switch hit my legs! She didn't even stop till blood was coming out of both legs. Junior was watching and was just shaking like a leaf on a tree.

She got done with me and looked at Junior, and he begin pushing his pant legs up.

She looked at him and said, "No, I'm not your Mom. Now you go in the house, and tell Otis to take you home and tell your Mom and Dad what you have done. Oh, and Junior I'll ask them if you left anything out.

Junior said as he took off, "I'll see you at school on Monday little Mac."

With that he was gone. She turned back to me and saw that the blood was getting my pant leg wet. "Here Little Mac, now sit down and eat this whole pack of smokes. ALL of them!"

I ate the whole pack of smokes, and threw up about ten times. Mom said "Alright little Mac, go in the house and put some medicine On the back of our legs. You're grounded for the whole weekend."

So that's the story of the burnt ends, and I never smoked again.

9

THE BOY

WITH A GIRL'S NAME

It was a cold afternoon in November of 1953, on Thanksgiving Day. An older lady impatiently paced the floor, while in the other room her daughter lay in bed in pain. The older lady is going to be my Grandma, and the lady in the other room is going to be my Mom, as soon as she gives birth today.

I'm Little Mac. Well I will be! Grandma let out a bad word, and said "Where is that man of yours? I'll bet he's behind the feed store in Leeper throwing dice and losing all his money! He needs to be here with you, you're having his kid!"

Mom replied "He will be here, I'm sure of it!"

Grandma was not going to wait, she opened the door and hollered out at my brother to get going to Leeper. And on the way, to stop and tell Dr. Pithy to get down here. "Your mother is laying here in pain, and she's getting really close. Then go behind the feed store, and tell your no-good daddy to get home right now!"

Kenny said, "Yes ma'am, I'm leaving right now!"

Mom said, "Don't ever let me hear you talk about their dad like that in front of the kids."

Grandma turned her head, and talked into her hands, "It's the truth, and the truth hurts!"

Then Grandma lifted her head from her hands. "You just watch and see, your man will come home drunk and broke! I'll bet my bottom dollar on that! Here you are with four kids and one on the way today, and he isn't even here!"

Mom was getting mad at her ma and dad both. So she said "Where's your man at, out with my man getting drunk too?"

Grandma said, "I'm not having a baby!"

Mom said, "No you have already had 15 kids, and he was out drunk on all of them I bet!"

It was just about a half an hour later when Dr. Pithy pulled up in his horse and buggy. He got a black bag from the back of the buggy and came through the front door. He asked, "How far apart are the contractions?"

Grandma replied, "About five minutes!"

Dr. Pithy told her, "Boil some water on the stove!"

Grandma told him, "Are you talking to me? if so, you better take that tone out of your voice right now, before I knock it out!"

Dr. Pithy asked again, "Would you please boil some water, Mrs. Laxton?"

She said, "Yes I will!"

Dr. Pithy went into the bedroom to check on me and Mom. "How are you doing Mrs. McFadden?"

She said, "I'm ready to get this baby out of me!"

At that time, my sister Kathy who was three and a half years old, turned over in the other bed and woke up crying."

"Mrs. Laxton would you take the baby in the front room please?" Dr. Pithy said to my Grandma.

Grandma came in from the kitchen, picked up Kathy and walked back out of the room without saying a word.

It was around 6:00 pm. When I was birthed, a little baby boy. Doc cleaned me up, give me to my Mom, and said, "A big boy, 8 pounds and 2 ounces."

Afterward, he pulled some paperwork out of his black bag. He asked Mom "What is this little boy going to go by?" Now Dr. Pithy was just a little hard of hearing, so that oughta explain what happened next. Mom said "His name is going to be Norman Bruce."

Doc said "Alright!" Thinking to his self, 'What a crazy name for a boy!" He turned to his paperwork and wrote the name Norma Bruce McFadden. He then turned back to my Mom and said, "If you need anything send one of the kids to get me. I'm going to be at the Johnson farm. One of the cows are going to have a baby sometime tonight."

See Dr. Pithy isn't a real Doctor at all, he is a veterinarian. But he is the closest thing to a Doctor that we had for miles.

It was about midnight when my finally Dad came in, about as quietly as a tree falling on the house! Just like Grandma said, he was drunk and broke.

I was the only turkey the McFadden family got that Thanksgiving, Nov. 22nd, 1953. An 8 pound 2 ounce boy, with a girl's name.

Note from the Author: This story was told by Little Mac's Grandmother. It is also noted that, shortly after Little Mac's birth, his Father's behavior changed greatly. He became a man well-liked and respected within the community, and was no longer known to drink or gamble. And while Little Mac's family was poor, in the sense that they had no money, they were very rich in the love they had from their Mom and Dad.

10

BUM'S CAVE

It's a beautiful day in the Spring of nineteen and thirty five. The sun is shining down on a small hill near the town of Mill Spring, Missouri. The flowers are blessing the hillside with beauty, the birds are singing theirs song of love. New life was blooming everywhere. In this little town, everything is right with the world.

Mr. Johnson was opening his little store, where he sold everything from horseshoes and hay bales, to milk and eggs. He had just walked to the back of the store to open up the side door. Some folks liked using the side door for some reason. The first to walk into the store was Ray and Eric.

They were two old men who sat at the back of the store playing checkers all day.

They had been there about an hour when Sheriff Thomson came in. It just so happened that Tom came in a minute later with something in his arms. Following right behind him was his only friend in the world, Billy. Billy was calling out to the Sheriff, "It's your niece, Sue!"

Sue was his brother's little girl, and she was only ten years old. The Sheriff met him half way, and took little Sue from Tom's arms. He ran to the back of the store where the old men were playing checkers. Mr. Johnson threw the checker board to the floor as the Sheriff lay little Sue on the table.

The Sheriff looked at Tom and Billy and said, "You two don't go anywhere. I'm going to get the Doctor. When I get back, you two got some questions to answer!"

Mr. Johnson did what he could to help little Sue, but he thought it was too late by the looks of it. He was afraid that she was already gone.

It took the sheriff about a half an hour to get back with the Doctor. As they came into the store, he told Ray to go and find Sue's dad. He looked at Tom and Billy and said, "You two come with me." He took them out to the front part of the store to talk with them.

"Tell me what happened." Said the Sheriff. "And start talking now!"

Tom spoke up. "Me and Billy was walking down the railroad tracks, and happened to look over by the spring. We saw one of them crazy hobos bending over little Sue. We hollered out, 'Hey you! what are you doing?'."

He looked up at us on the tracks, then he picked up a big rock and hit her right in the head with it. We ran down as fast as we could. By the time we got there, he was gone. Little Sue was lying on the grass with her pants down around her feet. I pulled them up and got her here as fast as I could.

The Sheriff, with a suspicious look on his face, asked Billy, "Have you got anything to add?"

Tom said, "He hasn't got anything to add sheriff."

"I would like to hear that from Billy!" Said the Sheriff.

"It happened just like Tom said." Replied Billy. He would never go against Tom on anything, because he knew what Tom was capable of doing to him.

About that time, Sue's dad Jimmy came in. "Where is my baby girl at Sheriff?"

"She's with the Doctor in back." The Sheriff told him.

"How is she?" Jimmy asked. "Go back and ask the doctor." said the Sheriff.

So Jimmy rushed to the back of the store. The Doctor looked at him and shook his head. Then he covered up Sue's face and turned to say, "Sorry, but she is gone."

Jimmy lay across her, crying, and said, "She was only ten, just a baby!"

The Doctor spoke to the sheriff, and said, "She was raped before she was killed."

Her dad Jimmy overheard what the doctor said. "Who found her?" He asked.

Tom said, "I did, and I saw who done it to her. It was one of those hobos from down at bums cave!"

-BACKSTORY: In the 1930's it was hard times for all, but for some it was harder. Men would leave their families and travel from town to town looking for work. They was called hobos and would stay in the cave right along the railroad tracks. It was home to as many as 20 hobos sometimes. But never the same ones. It was easy to get off and on the train, because it stops at a little station in the nearby town of Mill Spring.

Tom said, "Let's go down there and kill them all! Right now! They all just bums, who would care if we kill them all? We will get the right one!"

Jimmy said, "Okay, I'll go home and get my gun. Tom you get some rope and we will meet at the train station. We're gonna take care of all our problems at the same time!"

The Sheriff said, "I can't let you all do that!"

Jimmy grabbed his brother by the hand and pulled him back to where Sue was laid on the table. He pulled the cover from her little body. "Take a look brother, that was your beautiful niece! Now look at her face so beaten and bloody that you can hardly recognize her. She was only ten, and they raped her!"

The Sheriff looked up with a sad look on his face, and said, "I'm going to go out of town on a fishing trip, so do what you must. I won't be around to help you, or stop you." After that he walked out of the store, got in his car, and left.

It took about two hours for the men to meet at the train station. The sun was high in the sky. It was sometime around noon. Tom and Billy were the first to get there. Mr. Johnson came, and brought his gun with him. He had closed his store to take part in it. Ray and Eric had both gone home and got their guns, and joined the rest. They all started down the tracks to the cave.

Billy stopped to speak his mind. "Maybe we shouldn't do this Tom."

Tom pulled him to the side and told him, "If you don't start walking the track, I'll shoot you, tie your legs and throw you in the river!"With that Billy did not say another word. They kept on walking down the tracks.

Soon they arrived in the area of the cave. But when the men ran up the hill to the cave, Billy stayed on the tracks, looking at the Black River rolling down toward the south. He heard the gun shots, and could smell the gunpowder in the air. He never moved. He heard the cry from the hobos, and the shouting of the men at the hobos.

He looked up from the river, and could see an old black man coming down the hill from the cave. Tom was right behind him calling out, "Billy get him, he's getting away!"

But the old man stopped and fell at Billy's feet. "Help me, I didn't do anything!"

Billy looked him in the eyes and said, "I know you didn't." By that time Tom got there and put his gun to the back of the old man's head. When he shot him, the blood splattered on Billy face. Billy just stood there and watched as the town men dragged all the hobos to the river. They tied weights onto their legs, and threw them all into the river. After that, they all walked back the way they came. Billy sat there all day and watched the river roll on by.

It was two months later when Billy accidentally shot Tom on a hunting trip. Tom died. Two months after that, the sheriff got drowned on a fishing trip. Three months later, Ray was found hanging in his barn. Two days later Eric choked to death on a chicken bone. Mr. Johnson, a month later, was shot by a robber who came in through that side door that some of the folks liked to use. Jimmy, Sue's dad knew it wasn't right that all those men were killed. He just ended up putting a gun to his head and took his own life.

It was three years to the day after the massacre, that someone found a letter nailed to a tree. It was beside the river where the fifteen hobos had met their end. This is what the letter said: '*I Billy, need for all you to know the truth. I and Tom were walking down the train tracks and saw Sue picking flowers along the spring. He said look at Little Sue, she's growing up fast. I think I'll go down and get a kiss from her.*

So we walked down to talk to her, and Tom started hurting her. She tried to run away. Tom got her and pulled her to the ground, then he raped her. That's when a hobo from up on the tracks saw

*us and hollered at us. Before I knew what was
happening, Tom had picked up a rock and hit her
in the head two or three times. He get up and hit
me, and I fell to the ground. He got on top of me
and said 'If you tell anybody about what happened
here I'll cave your head in with a rock!'*

*I knew that he would too, so I kept my mouth
shut! It was all over, I had to kill every man who
took part in the hobos killing but one. That is me.
I'm going to tie a rock onto my legs, fall into the
river and let it roll me south.'*

They say at noon by the Black River along the
train tracks, on the patch going up the hill to a
lonely cave, You can still hear the cry of the
hobos. You can sometimes hear the shots of the
guns, and still smell the gunpowder in the air.

THE END

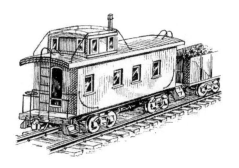

ABOUT THE AUTHOR

Norman Mcfadden is the President of The Glory Riders Motorcycle Ministry, based in Lincoln County Missouri. A former Pro Wrestler, Norman enjoys hunting and fishing, writing and his various works in Ministry.

ALSO FROM POLSTON HOUSE

AVAILABLE NOW

"Thomana did not look back. He knew that if he did, he would not go. He would stay and die with the woman he loved. But he could not give the baby over to this fate. He had promised."

Song doesn't know her dad's terrifying secret, and if she did, her entire world would come crashing down. Leigh is a simple woman leading a good life, but if her real past was revealed it just might kill her. When these two women are thrown together, everything they thought was real is shaken. Can they work with each other to survive, or will the one who has been searching for them achieve his hideous goal?

NORMAN MCFADDEN

ALSO FROM POLSTON HOUSE

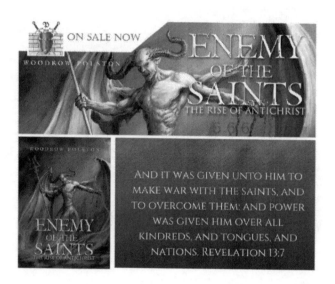

ON SALE NOW

ENEMY OF THE SAINTS
THE RISE OF ANTICHRIST

AND IT WAS GIVEN UNTO HIM TO MAKE WAR WITH THE SAINTS, AND TO OVERCOME THEM: AND POWER WAS GIVEN HIM OVER ALL KINDREDS, AND TONGUES, AND NATIONS. REVELATION 13:7

NORMAN MCFADDEN

Made in the USA
Lexington, KY
28 December 2018